ANGEL SPARKLE PUBLISHING

Magical
Fairy Land

COLORING BOOK FOR KIDS AND ADULTS

Did you have fun with this book?

★ ★ ★ ★ ★

Feel free to write us a review at
Amazon.com and share your pictures
with us. We really appreciate any
feedback.

Made in the USA
Las Vegas, NV
02 October 2022